SITTING IN SANDBOX

A rhyming book

Written by Molly Lovinggood
Illustrated by Katya Plaxina

I'm sitting in the sandbox,
and what do I see?

All of my toys just waiting for me!

Look at my boat

and buckets,
big and small.

My favorite is
a dump truck

full of sand
to haul.

I'm sitting in the sandbox,
and what do I see?

SALLY

Long ears a-flopping, a pair of droopy eyes,
on padded feet, she delivers my wet surprise.

Her long, pink tongue so sticky and wet,
makes my dog, Sally, the perfect pet!

A blue sky above is what I see,
as a pretty bird flies to a tree.

I'm sitting in the sandbox, and what do I see?
A bluebird sitting in the tree.

She's giving her baby birds
food to eat.
Soon, she'll fly away to find
another wormy treat.

I'm sitting in the sandbox and what do I see?
Our neighbor, Mr. Bill, waving at me.

He has a special job for each machine...

thin a tree,

whack a weed,

clip a hedge,

trim an edge.

No wonder his grass does not grow higher,
Mr. Bill and his machines never tire.

I'm sitting in the sandbox, and what do I see?
A smiling face that belongs to Mommy.

Without a fuss or tear, my sandbox
and I will part today.

But come tomorrow, I'll be back to play!

To John, James, Elizabeth, and Lucy
Remember to see the beauty!

Sitting in the Sandbox

ISBN: 978-0-9993089-0-5

Illustrations: Katya Plaxina, www.behance.net/katyapla

Book design: Peggy Nehmen, n-kcreative.com

For information about special sales, please contact: Molly Lovinggood, mollysbookshelf@gmail.com

Printed in the United States of America.

Reader Tips

The story uses two methods to help children learn reading skills. First, the repetition of "Sitting in the Sandbox" helps children anticipate story lines and what they may hear next. This is a great opportunity for learners to recognize letters, sounds, and words as they read the story on their own.

Second, the use of rhyming words helps children remember what they read. Take the opportunity to encourage children to read and repeat the sentence aloud. This reinforces letter and word recognition. Encourage learners to have fun making up more rhyming words … and to keep reading!

The hat of motherhood inspired **Molly Lovinggood** to write this story. She took such delight in watching her son explore his world that she wanted to share this story. Besides being a mother of 4, Molly was an elementary school educator for many years and has always been an avid nature lover. She and her husband currently reside in St. Louis, Missouri, with two black poodles.

Katya Plaxina loves making drawings for children books. Her focus is illustration for children's picture books, textbooks, character design for the animation and watercolor painting. She also works as a background artist at an animation studio.

Made in the USA
Lexington, KY
10 November 2017